To Dad, who loved being a grandpa—T.A.B.

To the Barron family,
with thanks for all their help,
and special recognition to Floyd Dickman
who believed in my artwork from the onset
of my career—C.K.S.

Patricia Lee Gauch, editor

Text copyright © 2000 by Thomas. A. Barron
Illustrations copyright © 2000 by Chris K. Soentpiet

Philomel Books, a division of Penguin Putnam Books for Young Readers,
345 Hudson Street, New York, NY 10014.
Philomel Books, Reg. U.S. Pat. & Tm. Off.
Published simultaneously in Canada
Printed in Hong Kong by South China Printing Co. (1988) Ltd.
Book design by Marikka Tamura and Patrick Collins. The text is set in Minion.
The artwork for this book was done with watercolor on illustration board.

Library of Congress Cataloging-in-Publication Data
Barron, T. A. Where is Grandpa? / T. A. Barron;
illustrated by Chris K. Soentpiet. p. cm.
Summary: As his family reminisces after his beloved grandfather's death,
a boy realizes that his grandfather is still with him in all the special places
they shared. [1. Grandfathers—Fiction. 2. Death—Fiction.
3. Grief—Fiction.] I. Soentpiet, Chris K., ill. II. Title.
PZ7.B27567Wh 2000 [E]—dc21 97-29549 CIP AC
ISBN 0 399-23037-8
10 9 8 7 6 5 4 3 2

Where is Grandpa?

BY **T. A. BARRON**

ILLUSTRATED BY **CHRIS K. SOENTPIET**

PHILOMEL BOOKS • NEW YORK

E<small>VERY</small> bird needs a nest,
and every kid needs a tree."
That's what Grandpa said
before he built my tree house
in the old cottonwood.
He knew how much I like
to climb trees.
Especially this tree.

Whenever Grandpa joined me
up there in the branches
he would say,
"Let's see as far as we can possibly see."
And I would look
beyond the horse pasture,
beyond the hills, all the way
to the Never Summer range
of the Rockies, and wonder
if somewhere up there
a young eagle was staring back at me.

Sometimes I climb up there
just to chatter with the squirrels.
Sometimes I climb up there
just to be alone.

To dream a little.

But not that day.
That day I didn't feel
like climbing. Or anything else.
You see, that was the day
Grandpa died.

For a long time I sat
on the porch step and waited.
When Dad came home
he got out of the car, moving slowly,
like an old man. Even older
than Grandpa.
Mom hugged him
for a long time. They came over
and sat beside me on the step.
My sister and brother joined us,
and for a while,
nobody spoke.

Then my sister started talking
about the time Grandpa took her
hiking in the hills above the ranch.
"When we rested by a creek,
he showed me how to hear
voices in the water,
low ones like drums pounding,
high ones like piccolos piping,
singing chorus or singing solo.
When we finally reached a waterfall
it was so loud that I heard it
before I saw it,
and it didn't look like water.
More like rainbows, pouring
over the cliff. Grandpa said
you could call it liquid light."
Dad looked up but said nothing.

My brother told about
the time Grandpa brought us
a whole passel of pumpkins.
"The kitchen was full of them,
all sizes and shapes.
We cooked pumpkin pie
and roasted pumpkin seeds,
and then we started to carve
wild faces, scary faces,
wacky faces, too. But best of all
was the pumpkin Grandpa carved,
with a hole in the bottom to fit
over his head. When he put
it on and met Mom at the door,
she screamed so loud
the cat lost eight lives."
Usually Dad laughed at that story,
but not this time.

Then Mom remembered
the first time she ever met Grandpa.
"He took me outside under the stars
and sat next to me
on the swing seat, the one he called
Creakybones.
We sat out there for hours,
the two of us,
talking about our childhoods—
his on a ranch by the Salmon River,
mine in a city by the Connecticut River."
She sighed.
"He made me feel so . . . comfortable."

At last Dad spoke up.
His voice sounded a long way off,
like an echo across a canyon.
"Once, when I was small,
he threw me onto his shoulders
and took me up into the hills.
Mist flowed everywhere,
so thick that sometimes I couldn't see
the red hair on his head.
Suddenly we stood face-to-face
with a ponderosa pine,
so enormous we could only reach
a little way around the trunk.
It had been dead
for at least fifty years, so it had
no bark and no leaves.
But it still stood tall, like the tower
of a ruined castle."

"Did you climb it?" I asked.
He looked past the porch step,
past Mom, past the wall
of our house.
"I climbed it, all right.
Up to a deep hole in the trunk.
That's where I found a whole family
of baby raccoons, all jumbled
together. I'll never forget their eyes,
brighter than lanterns."

Mom turned to me.
"What about you? Do you have
a story about Grandpa?"
Even if I did, I didn't feel
like telling it.
"Remember your camp-out in the
tree house?"
I shook my head.
"Or the horseshoe contest that
lasted three days?"
I shook my head again.
"Or the scarecrow you two made
out of snow?"
I shook my head again.

Dad touched my arm. "I miss him, too."
I drew a big breath. "There's something
I'm wondering about."
"What is it?"
"I'm not sure how to say it."
He suggested, "Just try."
"All right. Can anybody tell me . . .
Where is Grandpa now?"

Dad swallowed. "He's, well, gone now."

"But where?"

He thought for a moment. "I guess
you could say he's . . . in heaven."

"But where is that?"

"Well, heaven means different things
to different people.
And it's hard to explain."

I suggested, "Just try."
He glanced at Mom,
then turned back to me.
"Maybe you could say
that heaven is any place where
people who love each other
have shared some time together."
I thought about that idea.
"You mean . . .
like up there at the waterfall?
And by that old pine tree?
And maybe even in my tree house?"
He said nothing.
I leaned closer. "Heaven is in all
of those places?"
He nodded.
"So Grandpa is in all
of those places?"
A new look came over Dad's face, and
he almost smiled.

I thought about Grandpa
in all of those places.
And I almost smiled, too.
I knew it might be all right now
to climb the old
cottonwood. To stretch my arms.
To stretch my eyes all the way
to the Never Summer range
of the Rockies.

To see as far as I can possibly see.